Paw Prints
in the Snow

D1041537

Paw Prints
in the Snow

Sally Grindley

BLOOMSBURY

LONDON BERLIN NEW YORK SYDNEY

Bloomsbury Publishing, London, Berlin, New York and Sydney

First published in Great Britain in February 2012 by Bloomsbury Publishing Plc
50 Bedford Square, London, WC1B 3DP

Manufactured and supplied under licence from the Zoological Society of London

Text copyright © Sally Grindley 2012

The moral right of the author has been asserted

Licensed by Bright Group International
www.thebrightagency.com

With thanks to ZSL's conservation team

A CIP catalogue record for this book is available from the British Library

ISBN 978 1 4088 1945 6

MIX
Paper from
responsible sources
FSC® C018072
www.fsc.org

Typeset by Hewer Text UK Ltd, Edinburgh

Printed in Great Britain by Clays Ltd, St Ives plc, Bungay, Suffolk

3 5 7 9 10 8 6 4 2

www.storiesfromthezoo.com
www.bloomsbury.com
www.sallygrindley.co.uk

For Sasha Parris

Chapter 1

'What's it like putting your arm up a cow's bottom?' Joe Brook asked.

'Warm and squelchy.' Binti, his mother, grinned.

'You wouldn't catch me doing it.' Joe pulled a face.

He was standing on the bottom rung of some metal fencing inside a barn on Mike Downs's farm. His mother was the other side of the fence, dressed in her green overalls and wellington boots, her breath coiling upwards like steam from a kettle as she leant against the cow's rear. Joe watched as she pulled her arm out and removed the long plastic glove that covered most of it.

'It's not much fun for the cow, either,' she said.

'If I was going to be a vet, I'd only want to look after small animals like cats – or wild animals like elephants, because that would be cool.'

'So you think some of what I do is cool then, Joe?'

Binti smiled as she opened the gate and left the cow's enclosure. Most of her work was as an international wildlife vet, but when she was at home she sometimes helped out if called upon by other vets in the area.

'You might have to put your arm up an elephant's bottom too, you know,' she said.

'What for?'

'To find out if a female is pregnant, or perhaps to check for digestive problems. Pretty much the same as for a cow.'

'Well, I wouldn't mind so much if it was an elephant, because they're exciting and I'm half Tanzanian. Cows are boring.'

'Not to a bull they're not.' Binti laughed as she scrubbed her hands. 'Come on, it's dinner time.'

'I'm glad Dad does the cooking, knowing where your hands have just been.' Joe smirked.

His mother cuffed him gently.

Joe shivered as they left the barn. It had become dark and very chilly. They headed back towards the farmhouse, where Mike Downs greeted them on the doorstep. Through a window Joe could see a fire burning brightly and wished he were sitting in front of it.

'I can't find anything abnormal, Mike,' said Binti, 'but I'll send a stool sample off to the lab and see if they come up with anything. In the meantime, just keep an eye on her and give me a call if you're at all worried.'

'Thanks, Binti. I'll try not to disturb your weekend any further.'

'It's all part of the job, Mike. We can't expect animals to fall sick only on weekdays.'

'Are you going to follow in your mum's

footsteps when you're older, young man?' The farmer winked at Joe.

'My son doesn't like getting his hands dirty, do you, Joe?' Binti smiled. 'Right, we ought to make a move. Bye, Mike.'

She linked her arm through Joe's. They walked quickly over to their four-by-four and clambered in.

'Turn the heating up, Mum,' said Joe. 'It's got really cold.'

Binti switched on the engine and played with the dials. 'You'll have to get used to the cold where we're going,' she said, shooting him a glance to watch his reaction.

Joe looked puzzled. 'We're going home for dinner, aren't we?'

'But what about when you break up for half-term?' Binti questioned.

Joe detected a whiff of excitement. 'I know,' he said. 'We're going to Antarctica!'

'Not quite,' said Binti. 'But we *are* going to Russia.'

'Russia?' Joe wasn't sure how to react. 'Why are we going to Russia?'

'I'm going to help train some of the young vets over there in how to anaesthetize tigers.'

'But there aren't any tigers in Russia, are there?' said Joe. 'I thought they were all in India and Sumatra.'

'There are Amur tigers in Russia. They're the biggest, and there are very few left.'

Russia had sounded like a boring place to spend half-term – until Binti mentioned tigers. Now Joe couldn't think of anything better, even if it was going to be cold.

'I'll be working there for a month. You and Dad and Aesha will travel out with me and stay for eight days,' his mother explained. 'I know it's not for long, but you need to be back for school.'

When they arrived back home, Joe ran into the house, where Foggy, their schnauzer, rushed to greet him.

'Hey, Dad!' he called. 'Mum says we're going to Russia!'

'Does she indeed?' Peter Brook replied from the kitchen, where he was stirring a large pot of chilli beef. 'Just when I was thinking what a good idea it would be if there were the equivalent of boarding kennels for children for when their parents go away.'

'Only for annoying little nine-year-old boys.' A voice piped up from the next room. 'Not for beautiful, intelligent daughters.' Joe's thirteen-year-old sister, Aesha, followed him into the kitchen. 'I think that's a great idea,' she said. 'Boys could be left there until they're house-trained.'

'You're a fine one to talk about house-training, young lady,' said Binti. 'Your room's like a pigsty.'

'It's lived in, that's all.' Aesha pouted.

'You'll be living out if it gets much worse,' Binti replied.

'At least my room hasn't got piles of smelly socks and pants and soggy biscuits and crisps all over the floor,' said Aesha.

'It's got piles of clothes and shoes and lipsticks and photos instead.' Joe snorted.

'I rest my case,' said Peter. 'It would be far more peaceful for your mother and I if we went to Russia on our own. I'll speak to the doggery and see if they've got a spare compound.'

Chapter 2

Joe said his goodbyes to Foggy at Waggy Tails Boarding Kennels.

'Poor Foggy,' he bemoaned. 'He'll be lonely.'

'He'll be spoilt rotten,' said Binti.

'It seems cruel to go away and leave him,' said Joe.

'What, in a five-star boarding kennel in the lap of luxury? While we freeze our socks off, he'll be toasting his paws in front of that great log fire. I'm tempted to stay here myself,' Peter teased.

'Talking of which, I hope we've got enough warm clothes with us,' said Binti as Peter herded them back into the car.

'I'll look like a massive beluga whale in that coat you bought me,' grumbled Aesha. 'And I refuse to wear that silly hat.'

'I'll *eat* my hat if you manage not to wear yours!' chuckled Peter as he turned on the ignition.

'Don't encourage her!' Binti chided.

'Don't wear it, Aesha!' shrieked Joe. 'You'll look more ridiculous than usual if you do.'

'Ha, funny, ha.' Aesha scowled.

Peter began to sing the lyrics from *Winter Wonderland*, adopting a deep, bass voice that they all tried to copy, chins pulled into their necks, their expressions like a bulldog's, until Joe began to splutter from the effort. Aesha, blushing, adopted a sophisticated pose on spotting a group of boys in a car that was overtaking them.

'Why did they change the name of Siberian tigers to Amur tigers?' she asked, though she already knew the answer.

'Amur is more accurate, since that's the part of Russia where they're found,' Binti replied.

'It's funny how some tigers live in really hot places, like India, and others live in really cold places,' remarked Joe.

'But that's just like people,' said Aesha rather scornfully.

'People can wear different clothes depending on the weather,' Joe persisted. 'Tigers have fur coats wherever they live.'

'They'd look funny if they were bald,' chipped in Peter.

'Like you, Dad,' chuckled Aesha.

'Joe's making a good point,' said Binti. 'We would wear fur in the cold, but not in the heat.'

'*We* wouldn't wear fur at all,' said Aesha, 'unless it was fake.'

'So tigers in India probably have very sweaty armpits,' observed Peter. 'Or should that be leg-pits?'

'In fact,' said Binti, 'Amur tigers have thicker coats than Indian tigers, as well as a fold of fat running along their bellies to help keep them warm.'

'Is that why Dad's got a fold of fat running along his belly?' chortled Joe.

'I have not!' Peter protested. 'Bald I might be, but fat I am not.'

'At least you'll be warm.' Binti turned to grin at him.

'It's a conspiracy,' he huffed. 'I knew I should've stayed at the doggery.'

'What exactly are we supposed to do while we're in Russia?' asked Aesha.

'I'll be photographing anything that moves for a magazine article, and I expect you, my princess, will sit by the fire, filing your nails and looking beautiful,' replied Peter.

'I'm going to help Dad,' said Joe proudly. His parents had bought him a camera for his birthday and he was keen to follow in his father's footsteps.

'I'm sure there'll be plenty to keep you amused,' Binti told Aesha.

Aesha frowned. She was excited about going to Russia, but she hated the cold even more than Joe did, and couldn't imagine that there would be much to do in a place where it might snow even though it was only late October, and where the temperatures could drop well below zero.

'I know about the tigers and the brown bear, but what other animals are there in eastern Russia?' Joe asked.

'There are more animals and birds than you would imagine,' said Peter, 'though many will be in hibernation. For starters, there's the Himalayan black bear, the Siberian chipmunk, the Amur goral, Blakiston's fish owl, scaly merganser, hooded crane, Japanese blue-and-yellow-rumped flycatcher, wild boar, Manchurian sika …'

'Someone's been doing their homework.' Binti smiled, impressed.

'Of course,' said Peter.

'What's a goral?' asked Joe.

'It's a sort of cross between a goat and an antelope,' offered Binti.

When they arrived at the airport, Peter parked the car at a drop-off point and they all piled out. A valet was waiting, ready to take their car away to a long-stay car park.

'Going somewhere hot?' he asked.

Chapter 3

Joe kept himself occupied during the long flight. He watched two films, slept a bit, ate the rather overcooked meal that was put in front of him, jumped from one game on his console to another, played cards with his father and listened to music. He looked on with amusement as a large man across the aisle made himself comfortable, closed his eyes and began to snore. The man's head dropped forward occasionally, swayed from side to side with the movement of the aircraft, then jolted backward again as if an electric shock had been administered.

'He sounds like a walrus, doesn't he, Dad?' Joe whispered, nudging his father.

'I have no personal experience of walruses, but if you say so then I'll take your word for it,' Peter whispered back.

At that moment the man snorted loudly and the magazine that had been resting on his belly fell to the floor. Joe bent down to pick it up and was upset to see that it had a photograph of a dead tiger on the cover. A man with a gun held high stood triumphantly by its head. Joe couldn't read the caption because it was written in what he took to be Russian.

'Give the gentleman his magazine back, Joe,' Peter prompted.

Joe turned to see that the man had woken and was looking questioningly at him. He thrust the magazine towards him as if it were burning his fingers. The man said something gruffly, pushed the magazine into the seat pocket and closed his eyes again.

'Did you see that, Dad?' Joe whispered after

a while. 'There was a dead tiger on the cover of his magazine. I knew he looked a bit fishy.'

'Walruses are,' said Peter.

'That's not funny,' Joe growled.

'Having a dead tiger on your magazine doesn't make you fishy,' Peter whispered. 'Your mum's always surrounded by pictures of animals, dead and alive, and she's not fishy – thank goodness. I never did see myself marrying a mermaid.'

'But Mum's an international wildlife vet,' Joe said hotly.

'So might the Walrus be,' replied Peter.

Joe didn't think for one minute that the large grumpy man across the aisle was an international vet. He wanted to ask his mother what she thought, but Binti and Aesha were both snuggled up in their blankets, fast asleep. Joe tried to go to sleep as well, but he couldn't help casting sideways glances at his neighbour, and the more he studied him, the more he convinced himself that the man was some sort of villain. *He might be a hunter, or a poacher, or a smuggler of tiger parts!*

Binti had told him about how valuable tiger parts were in some societies, and he knew the skins were worth a fortune. He also knew that trading in tiger parts was strictly illegal.

I bet that's what he does, Joe thought, only to see that the man had woken up again and was delving into a packet of sweets. Joe watched out of the corner of his eye as he put a sweet in his mouth and began to suck on it. The man suddenly held the packet across the aisle and encouraged Joe to take one. Joe shook his head and moved nearer his father. He did his best to ignore the man for the rest of the flight.

When they landed in Moscow, he kept close to Binti as they trekked along the airport's endless corridors until they reached the lounge reserved for passengers waiting for connecting flights. They had a long wait, and Joe was annoyed to discover that the man had followed them.

'Are you tired, Joe?' Binti asked, putting her arm around his shoulders. 'You look done in.'

Joe shrugged. He *was* tired, but he didn't want to admit it. 'What happens to people who get caught smuggling tiger parts?' he asked.

'Not enough, frankly,' Binti replied. 'It's not considered that serious an offence by some courts, though it seems to me that anyone profiting from the potential extinction of any form of wildlife should have the book thrown at them.'

'I bet they're not very nice, the people who do that,' said Joe.

'In some cases that's probably true,' said Binti. 'In other cases it's more complicated. We can't necessarily blame people for seizing the few opportunities that come their way to climb out of poverty. In those cases we need to help them find other ways to earn a living.'

'But tigers are dying out,' Joe protested.

'And that's why so many caring people all over the world are doing everything they can to save them.'

Joe looked across at the man who was now sitting at a table in the transit lounge café. 'What would you do if you thought someone might be a smuggler?'

'I'd try to find some evidence and then report them to the authorities,' said Binti. 'But it's not easy – it's not as if they have "smuggler" written across their foreheads.'

Joe thought about the one piece of 'evidence' he had had – the magazine. It didn't amount to very much – nothing at all, if he was honest with himself. He would just have to forget the man.

He was relieved when at last they boarded the onward flight to Vladivostok, but dismayed to see that the man was boarding it too.

Chapter 4

'It's freezing!' Aesha cried, as they hurried towards the minibus that was waiting for them outside the terminal at Vladivostok airport.

'Isn't that what we were expecting?' Her father grinned.

'There's freezing and then there's freezing. This is *f-f-f-freeeeezing*!'

'Put your hat on then!' said Binti.

'It's not that bad,' Aesha replied quickly, scrambling into the minibus while the driver stowed their luggage in the back. 'It's warm in here. Hurry up and get in!'

'You're right about one thing – you do look

like a beluga,' chirped Joe, jumping into the seat behind her so that she couldn't take a swipe at him.

They set off through the town. Joe found himself gripping the door handle as the minibus swerved past cars that were going too slowly along sweeping boulevards lined with buildings that seemed to belong to another century. The next minute, they were driving nose to tail through streets that were too narrow for all the traffic. The driver was very vocal and shook his fist at anyone he deemed to be in his way.

'He's excitable,' Peter observed.

'He's a lunatic!' Binti muttered.

Joe stared with fascination when they passed close to the harbour because he loved looking at boats. Small private yachts were moored next to trawlers and cargo ships, while passenger liners were busily swapping places with ferry boats and a huge tanker drifted along the horizon. The road continued to follow the seafront, skirting an extensive stretch of sandy beach.

'I never thought of Russia being by the sea,' Joe said.

'You wouldn't catch me swimming in it,' Aesha declared.

'People do, in the summer. The temperatures then are similar to ours in the UK,' Binti told her.

'So it's not that warm,' scoffed Aesha.

Soon after they turned inland it began to snow lightly and Binti expressed her concern that they might not make it to Lazovsky, where they were heading.

'Don't worry,' said Peter brightly. 'Russia doesn't come to a standstill like it does back home just because of a bit of snow.'

Joe gazed out at the whitening world, feeling excited. This was proper snow – great big flakes the size of cottonwool balls were dropping from the sky, and every mile they travelled took them closer to the realm of the Amur tiger. He peered intently at the pine woods fringing the highway. *I'd so love to see a tiger in the wild*, he thought. His mother, however, had warned him that the chances were almost nil.

'I'm sure you'll be able to watch any camera footage that's shot while we're there, but you won't be allowed to join the night patrols,' said Binti, as if reading his mind. 'The most you can hope for is that we spot a tiger when we're driving around the reserve, but there are so few of them left.'

'How many?' Aesha wanted to know.

'In the area we're visiting, only about ten. In total, in Russia, around four hundred.'

'No wonder there's such a big campaign to save them,' Aesha pondered. 'It would be a crime if they became extinct.'

Joe continued to scour the woodlands and fields as they progressed. *Even if I don't see a tiger, I might spot something else while everyone is dozing*, he thought to himself.

Joe must have fallen asleep, though, because the next thing he knew, someone was shaking his shoulder.

'Wake up, sweet prince,' Peter said. 'We've arrived at our castle.'

Joe struggled to open his eyes. He was disappointed to find it was nearly dark outside, and even more disappointed to discover that their 'castle' was a rather grim-looking hotel. His mother and Aesha were in the lobby, being welcomed by a woman dressed in a big furry hat and a deeply quilted coat, who spoke English with a heavy accent. Joe shivered. It was only a few short steps into the hotel, but he was reluctant to leave his cocoon. He pulled his own coat around him, jumped down from the minibus and looked about.

Everywhere was covered with a thin layer of snow. Joe had hoped it would be deeper. He wanted it to be so deep that he would have to lift his feet up to his ears just to walk through it! There had been a lot more snow back home the previous winter, when everyone had talked about the snowfalls as being among the heaviest on record.

'How long are we staying in this place?' he asked as they walked through the dimly lit hotel lobby.

'Only till the morning. We arranged for a stopover here because it's so late. We, and our hosts in Lazo, felt it would be better if we set off tomorrow, refreshed and in daylight.' Binti smiled at him. 'Don't worry,' she said. 'I know two days of travelling isn't much fun, but the adventure is about to begin!'

Joe nodded as she squeezed his shoulder. He was overwhelmed with tiredness and right at that moment would have been happy to sleep anywhere – even standing up, there in the lobby. He allowed his eyes to close briefly. When he opened them again, he noticed the man from the plane, the Walrus, sitting on a stool in the hotel bar.

Chapter 5

Early the next morning, the Brooks prepared to set off on the final leg of their journey. Joe had slept well despite his sighting of the Walrus. At breakfast, an unexciting affair of a kind of bread called *kleb* and processed cheese, he watched for him to appear, but there was no sign of him.

They were collected by the manager of the research centre in Lazo, a brisk, athletic-looking woman in her thirties called Iona Petrov. She shepherded them into a six-seater car and asked them to wait while she disappeared back into the hotel. A few seconds later, she came out again with the man from the plane, who loaded his luggage into the back of the car.

'This is Artem Klopov,' she introduced him. 'He works with us as a dog handler. He's just come back from a training course in the UK. He doesn't speak much English, though he understands more.'

Artem Klopov nodded to them and clambered awkwardly into the front of the car.

Grinning broadly, Peter turned round to Joe and muttered, 'Very fishy'.

Joe was annoyed that he had voiced his suspicions, and a little dismayed at being deprived of his imagined role as detective. He stared out of the window and began to wonder what sort of work a dog handler would be doing at the tiger station. He even found himself wondering if dog-handling was just a cover for Artem Klopov's activities as a smuggler, before he scolded himself for being ridiculous.

The final part of their journey took just three hours, during which time Iona chatted to Binti about her team's work with tigers and discussed how they were educating the local community in the importance of conservation.

'This is a society that has hunting ingrained in it, so we have to change the traditional mindset. The problem is not just that tigers are being poached, but that the animals they feed on are declining in number. Tigers can't survive if there isn't enough food, and on top of that, all the animals are being seriously affected by illegal logging, which is destroying their habitat.'

Iona chatted with Artem too. Joe wished he could understand what they were saying. Peter asked her a question about Artem's work, and they learnt that it involved training a team of dogs to recognise different scents.

'Sniffer dogs are invaluable in helping us track tiger movements in the Lazovsky Nature Reserve,' Iona translated. 'It's a new and vital part of our operation.'

Joe was intrigued. He hoped he would get a

chance to watch the sniffer dogs at work, and decided that Artem must be a decent person after all if he was involved in tiger conservation.

'You'll be spending most of your time at our park headquarters, and we've arranged for you to stay within the reserve for a couple of nights. How does that sound?' Iona looked in her mirror to observe her passengers' reactions.

'Cool!' said Joe. *Staying inside the reserve sounds like the starting point of an adventure to me.*

'Sounds perfect to me,' said Peter.

'Our headquarters are a little bit basic, but at least by staying there you'll feel as though you're properly involved.'

'I hope the heating works,' Aesha said wryly.

'The heating is good, very good,' Iona replied. 'The electricity is not so good.'

'No television, then, eh, Joe?' Peter observed.

Joe shrugged. 'I don't mind,' he said. 'I'm going to be out taking photos with you.'

'And what sort of thing do you like to photograph?' asked Iona.

Joe didn't really know yet, so he said quickly, 'Well, anything that moves, mostly.'

'He's following in his father's footsteps,' Peter said with a chuckle.

'This trip should give you plenty of scope for that.' Iona laughed. 'What about you, Aesha? Whose footsteps are you following in?'

'I'm creating my own unique trail,' Aesha replied loftily.

'You can say that again,' Binti remarked. 'It's comprised of hairbands, make-up, shoes and sweet papers from one end of the house to the other.'

'Mum!' Aesha protested.

Binti smiled at her. 'What my daughter won't tell you herself is that she's a very talented swimmer and hopes to swim for England one day.'

'What she also won't tell you, because she doesn't realise it herself, is that she's very artistic,' Peter added. 'And Joe, I think, will wind up working with animals like his mum, however much he pretends he dislikes getting his hands dirty, on top of being an ace photographer.'

'So much talent all round!' Iona exclaimed. 'And here we are at last. Welcome to Lazovsky. I hope we can make this trip a very special one for you.'

Chapter 6

The snow hadn't reached the coastal village of
Lazo. A uniform greyness clung to the painted
wooden houses that lined the road, which were
interspersed with faceless apartment blocks. On
one side, they drove past a ferry that was unload-
ing two cars on to a muddy landing stage. A little
further on, Joe spotted an old dilapidated bus that
he assumed had been abandoned, though he later
saw it trundling along full of passengers. On the
other side, there were a couple of shops and a café,
before Iona pointed out the Museum of Nature.

'The museum's very important to us,' Iona
said. 'We have lots of activities there to show

local people the work we're doing, what our objectives are and how they can help us. We're especially keen to involve children, because they're the future. We recently ran a tiger painting competition and some of the paintings were brilliant – the best ones are still on show inside. And there's a fantastic butterfly collection.'

Joe wished he'd been able to enter the competition and resolved to do his own painting while they were in Lazo. He wondered if they might display it in the museum if it was good enough. It would be better still if he could take a photograph of a tiger! *If only*, he thought.

They pulled up outside a large concrete building.

'This is it,' said Iona. 'This is where we live and work, and where you'll be staying for some of the time.' She warned them again that it was rather basic. 'The towels aren't very fluffy, and you might need to resort to head torches, which we'll supply you with, if the electricity is playing up.'

Joe quite liked the idea of wearing a head torch – he could imagine he was a miner – though he could tell from Aesha's face that she wasn't so happy. She was even less happy when they were shown to their rooms – she and Joe were in one, their parents in the other. The walls were rough, unpainted concrete, the furniture was old and rickety, and the towels were indeed threadbare.

'We've got more fluff on our tea towels at home!' she exclaimed. 'How do the people who work here live like this? Why don't they make it nicer?'

'As Iona explained, all the money they're given goes towards efforts to save the tigers,' Binti replied. 'I think you'll find that the people who work here are so dedicated they scarcely notice their surroundings. And this is far better than the tents they sometimes have to sleep in in the middle of the *taiga*.'

'What's the *taiga*?' asked Joe.

'It's a type of forest with mostly coniferous trees, like spruce and pine.'

'They wouldn't sleep there in a tent in the winter, though, would they?' Aesha said.

'Oh yes, they would,' Binti replied. 'One of the experts slept in a tent in the snow for two weeks, even when the temperature went down to minus twenty-five. He said he got used to it.'

'That's impossible!' cried Aesha. 'He must be mad!'

'You should see some of the places I've stayed in for the sake of the perfect photo,' said Peter. 'I've waited up trees, in caves, on roofs, in the middle of a desert. I suppose that means I'm mad too.'

'Yes, Dad, you are,' said Aesha. 'Barking.'

'Woof, woof.' He put his arm around his daughter's shoulder. 'You know it's catching, don't you?'

'What about my training?' she interjected. 'I can't believe it – we're right next to the sea but I can't jump in the water.'

Aesha had an important competition coming up a few weeks after their return to England and was anxious about being ready for it. She had trained really hard right up until the day before they left, and although Binti had assured her that most of the other competitors would relax a little over half-term, Aesha was not convinced.

'If you were Russian you might give it a go,' her father observed.

'If I were mad I might!'

'It's catching.' Joe chuckled.

'I've read about the people who do,' said Binti. 'They call themselves "*morzhi*", or "walruses", and they jump into freezing cold lakes to welcome in the new year.'

'Ha! We're back to walruses again, Joe.' Peter laughed.

Joe blushed and dug his father in the ribs.

'Do you think there'll be a pool somewhere close by?' Aesha asked.

Binti looked doubtful. 'I can check, but unless there's one in the village there won't be any way of getting you there.'

'A few dogs and a sledge?' Peter suggested.

'It's a bit of a dump, this place, isn't it?' Aesha was decidedly grumpy. 'I can't see us having much fun here.'

Joe had a few doubts himself. From what he had seen of the towns they had driven through and the village itself, it all looked rather bleak, but he picked up on his father's comment.

'Do you think we might be able to go on a sledge?' he asked.

'This is your mother's trip, Joe,' Peter replied. 'The timetable will be set by what she needs to achieve.'

'And I might have a few surprises up my sleeve,' said Binti. 'Wait and see what tomorrow brings.'

Chapter 7

Joe and Aesha needn't have worried. Iona and her team members had arranged a full programme for them.

'We thought you might be bored, and we want to make sure you leave our country with some great memories,' she said with a big smile. 'And of course we want you to have an understanding of the work we do. It's important that there are youngsters eager to take over from us when we're old and decrepit.'

While Binti met up with members of the tiger team to discuss their latest activities and results, and while Peter made plans to photograph various aspects of their work, Joe and Aesha were collected by jeep and asked if they would like to help train a group of sniffer dogs.

'Yes, please!' said Aesha immediately.

Joe was thrilled at the idea of training the dogs, but a little bit embarrassed. After all the suspicious thoughts he had had about Artem Klopov, was he actually going to help him, or would it be someone else? *At least it'll give me a chance to make amends*, he thought.

It was only a short ride to the kennels, which backed on to a single-storey wooden building with offices. Artem Klopov greeted them with a gruff smile and a bone-crunching handshake.

'Welcome,' he said with a very heavy accent, and indicated that they should follow him.

He led them along a narrow corridor towards a heavy door at the far end. They could hear the odd muffled bark coming from beyond it. Joe was reminded of Foggy and hoped he was being well looked after. Once they were through the door, the barking became a cacophony of excitement with each dog vying for attention. There were five of them, all black, individually penned in brick-walled kennels with wire-mesh fronts and a high gate in the middle. Artem called out something in Russian and as one they stopped barking and sat. Joe and Aesha looked at each other in amazement. Artem grinned.

'Better!' he said, in English this time.

Joe nodded. 'Much better,' he agreed.

Artem pointed to each of the dogs in turn and called out their names – Ivan, Ilya, Nika, Boris and Tanya – before producing a packet of biscuits for Joe and Aesha to feed them with.

'Not Ivan,' he said. 'Ivan work now.'

He opened the door to Ivan's enclosure and ordered him out. Ivan looked up appealingly at the packet of biscuits. Aesha laughed at his eager face and fondled his ears, until Artem ordered the dog to follow him as he strode off along a further stretch of corridor. They went through another door, which opened into a big room that was empty apart from a table against one of the walls. A few seconds later, a young woman carrying several boxes and a pile of plastic cones came into the room. She put the boxes on the table and introduced herself as Nadia.

'I'm a student and I'm working on the Tiger Project. I'm pleased to meet with the children of an eminent vet like Doctor Binti Brook.'

Joe felt a tingle of pride at hearing what she thought of his mother.

'We begin,' said Artem. 'Cones, Nadia.' He called Ivan to heel.

Nadia gave ten cones to Joe and asked him to put them in a large circle. Joe placed them very carefully, keen to please.

'Now scat,' said Artem.

Joe and Aesha looked at each other in surprise. *Is that it? Is that all we're going to be allowed to do? Have we somehow upset Artem?* Joe wondered.

He began to move towards the door. Aesha was rooted to the spot, looking puzzled.

'Where you go?' Artem asked.

Joe stopped, confused.

'Here scat.' Artem held a box out to Joe and pointed to one of the cones. 'Put under.' He held a second box out to Aesha and indicated another of the cones. Joe took his box and hurried to the cone. He bent down and was about to place it underneath when Nadia interrupted him.

'No, Joe, the scat is in the box,' she said. 'Take the lid off the box.'

'What's scat?' Aesha asked.

'Ah, you don't know? Scat is tiger faecal matter.' Nadia smiled, watching their blank faces. 'Otherwise known as tiger poop.'

Aesha promptly held the box she had been given as far away from herself as possible. 'Yuck!' she exclaimed.

Joe was more curious. He slowly took the lid off his box and stared at the contents. Artem gave a deep belly laugh.

'Much fur,' he said.

It was true. The piece of scat was hairy and

quite dry. Joe quickly placed the box under the cone and asked Aesha if she wanted him to take hers. She shook her head vehemently.

'I'm not a baby,' she muttered, before opening her box distastefully and placing the scat under the designated cone.

'Good,' said Artem. 'These now.'

He handed out more boxes to Joe, Aesha and Nadia to position the scat wherever they wished under the remaining cones.

'Is good,' he said when they had finished. 'Now Ivan turn.'

He held an open box containing a scat sample under Ivan's nose, then withdrew it, replaced the lid and put it on the table. Next he led Ivan to the middle of the circle and told him to sit. Ivan obeyed and waited there patiently while Artem walked back to the edge of the room.

'Your sample the same,' he said to Joe and Aesha, pointing to the box on the table.

'The first samples you were given to place under the cones are both from the same tiger, and so is the one Ivan has just sniffed,' Nadia helped to explain. 'He has to find the two that are the same among the ones that come from different tigers.'

'Can he really do that?' Joe asked incredulously.

'Very good nose,' said Artem, pointing to his own nose. He called out an instruction to Ivan.

The dog leapt to his feet and ran to each of the cones in turn. He stopped by the first cone Joe had placed, walked round it, sniffing continuously, then sat down right next to it.

'Good dog, Ivan,' Nadia cried, and sent him back to the cones.

Ivan sniffed out the second scat in no time and sat down next to the cone, wagging his tail vigorously.

'He's so clever!' said Aesha. 'Two out of two!'

'Two poos out of two.' Joe giggled.

'Will he get a reward for being so good?' Aesha asked.

'We reward the dogs with play sessions,' Nadia replied. 'They have so much fun.'

Artem asked them to shuffle the cones around while Ivan was taken out of the room. When he returned Ivan was sent to find the correct scats again. Yet again, he was right both times.

'Best dog,' said Artem.

One by one, the dogs were put through their paces, some more successfully than others. Joe darted about, shifting cones, replacing scats and leading the dogs back to their pens when their turn was over. Aesha helped Nadia to bring the dogs out and settle them down before their test. Artem painstakingly recorded the results and left Nadia to explain the purpose of their work.

'If the dogs can identify different tigers from their scats it will help us to keep track of how many different tigers there are in the area. It'll also alert us to the absence of a particular tiger if we suddenly can't find any trace of it.'

'But how can the dogs tell the difference?' Joe asked.

'We're not really sure,' said Nadia, 'but it seems there may be unique features to the scat of individual tigers, just as individual people have different scents.'

Joe was sorry when their time with the dogs came to an end and a jeep arrived to take Aesha and him back to the lodge. They thanked Artem and Nadia, who gave each of them a tiny bronze tiger to take away as a memento.

'We've had a brilliant day,' Aesha said to their mother as soon as she saw her.

'We've spent the day playing with tiger poo!' chuckled Joe.

'Whoever would have thought it.' Binti smiled.

'And look what they gave us.' Joe showed Binti his tiger. 'I'm going to treasure this for ever,' he said. 'It'll always remind me of those amazing sniffer dogs.'

Chapter 8

The following day, the Brook family packed their things ready to leave for the heart of the Lazovsky Nature Reserve. This was what Joe had been waiting for – the chance to see a tiger in the wild. It didn't matter how many times he was told that it was extremely unlikely, he was convinced he would be lucky.

'Mum says most of the people who work here have never seen one, so why do you think *you*'re going to?' Aesha asked him.

Joe shrugged. 'Someone has to,' he said rather lamely.

A horn sounded outside and it was time to go. They piled into Iona's jeep.

'How were the dogs?' she asked as they set off.

'So clever!' said Aesha.

'It was fun,' said Joe, 'especially when Boris knocked all the cones over. He was very naughty.'

'Ah, poor Boris. He is a little slow on the uptake and might not make it as a sniffer dog, but he's my favourite,' said Iona. 'Today, you see more of our work – our real work – and tomorrow too. Tomorrow you'll be able to come with us while we check some of our camera traps.'

'Traps?' Aesha was alarmed. 'Why do you set traps?'

'They're not traps in the real sense of the word,' her father explained. 'The project workers have set up cameras in areas where tigers are known to roam. If a tiger walks into the camera's range, its movement will activate the camera to start filming the tiger.'

'We can identify individual tigers by their stripes,' Iona continued. 'It's another way of keeping track of how many different tigers there are in the region.'

'Wow! So will we be able to watch the films?' Joe asked.

'We might not find anything on them, but if we do then, yes, of course you will,' Iona reassured him.

'It won't just be tigers that are filmed, will it?' said Aesha. 'There'll be other animals as well.'

'Anything that moves at the right height and proximity will trigger the camera,' said Peter.

'So we might see bears?' Joe was thrilled at the thought.

'We're more likely to see the common species, like deer and wild boar,' said Iona. 'Though we did have some beautiful shots of a Himalayan black bear once.'

Joe knew he would be excited if they found anything at all, though tigers or bears would be the best as far as he was concerned. 'It would be so cool if we saw a tiger cub,' he said to Aesha.

'I'd love to see a tiger cub,' Aesha said wistfully, 'especially a really tiny one.'

'They are rather cute,' said Iona, 'but there's very little chance of that, sadly. Remember, only ten to twelve tigers have been regularly recorded in this nature reserve, and very young cubs stay in the warmth of their dens.'

Joe stared out of the window. *Only ten to twelve tigers hidden in all the dense forest and snow-covered mountains that surround us . . .*

'There are no fences to stop the tigers wandering out of the reserve, either,' Iona added, 'so at times the number may be even lower.'

'But that means tigers from elsewhere can come in too,' Aesha observed.

'And that's what can make it exciting.' Iona nodded. 'Especially when a young tiger we've never seen before appears.'

'Just like the two of you appearing out of the

blue,' Peter joked. 'It must have made Iona's day.'

'Oh, Dad!' Aesha protested.

They were approaching the entrance to the reserve. Joe gazed beyond, expecting that it would look different somehow, but it looked just the same as on the outside.

'We're very privileged, you know,' said Peter. 'Normally access to the reserve is restricted to scientists, fieldworkers and forest rangers.'

'But we're going to be acting as fieldworkers, aren't we, Dad?' said Joe. 'And Mum's a scientist.'

'You're very welcome anyway.' Iona laughed. 'A trip inside the reserve is the least we can offer, given that your mother is helping train some of our young vets.'

'Why do they have to be trained to deal with tigers if they'll never come across one?' asked Aesha.

'You can never say never,' said Binti, which made Joe smile. 'But it's not just tigers — it's wildlife in general. The vets need to be trained how to take samples from the animals tigers feed on. If those animals are carrying disease, it will spread to the tigers. Healthy prey, healthy tigers.'

Joe was proud his mother knew so much that she could train other vets, even those who were living on the other side of the world. Now that they were finally inside the reserve, he stared out of the window hoping to be the first to spot an animal of any sort, or at least its tracks.

He wasn't quick enough. Iona's trained eyes soon picked out a sika deer, screened by trees, eating the leaves from a low bush. She also pointed to a Siberian thrush and a yellow-throated meadow bunting, and soon after that she showed them the tracks of a wild boar.

'Your eyesight must be amazing,' Joe exclaimed.

'I'm sure at your age yours is better.' Iona smiled. 'But I know where to look. Let's stop soon and get out – we can't take the jeep very far into the forest and you'll see more on foot.'

'Isn't it dangerous?' Aesha sounded anxious.

'Less dangerous than crossing a road,' Iona assured her.

'But what if a tiger comes?' Joe asked, though he was incredibly excited about walking where tigers walked.

Peter laughed. 'There's probably more chance of seeing a bus.'

Chapter 9

Joe thought the hike was brilliant. They warmed up in no time, so much so that they wound up carrying their coats even though there was a smattering of snow on the ground. Because of their presence, there was little sign of wildlife, but there were plenty of birds flitting from tree-top to treetop and Peter was determined to photograph as many species as possible. Joe tried as well, but his camera wasn't powerful enough to produce anything more than indecipherable shadows that could just as easily have been leaves as birds. Peter took to photographing trees too, much to Joe's amusement.

'I thought you were going to photograph anything that moved,' he chortled. 'Trees don't move.'

'They sway in the wind,' his father countered, 'and they're home to all the birds I've been photographing. Anyway, I'm being very arty with my close-ups of the bark.'

Joe looked at the latest shot on the LCD screen of his own camera and wished he could be as creative. Then he spotted something in the background that even Iona hadn't seen.

'Look. What's that?' he asked. 'There's a face behind that bush.'

Peter and Iona stared hard at the camera screen.

'Well, well!' Iona exclaimed at last. 'You've captured a roe deer and he's posing beautifully for you!'

'Fluke!' scoffed Aesha.

'Pure skill,' said Joe.

He was proud of himself, even if he hadn't known the deer was there at the time. He smiled at the thought of looking at another photograph and discovering a tiger winking at him in the background.

Iona knew the reserve like the back of her hand and took them to several spectacular view-points. She had brought a picnic lunch with her, which they stopped close by a waterfall to eat.

'I can't believe we're eating a picnic in the snow in the middle of a forest in Russia!' said Aesha.

'Where Amur tigers live!' added Joe enthusiastically.

'Poor Joe,' said Binti. 'I wish we could magic up a tiger for you, but I think you're going to have to wait till we go home and visit the zoo.'

'I've seen tigers in the zoo, but it's not the same as seeing them in the wild,' Joe replied.

'Zoos do very important work in helping to protect them in the wild,' said Binti. 'Without that work – not just in our country but overseas as well – tigers might have become extinct already.'

'It seems cruel to keep them cooped up in a zoo just so that people can go and stare at them, though,' said Aesha.

'If you don't engage people's interest, you won't have their support when it comes to raising funds to save an endangered species,' Binti explained.

'And zoos enable scientists to study animals at first-hand. Many of the animal species in reputable zoos are endangered. The role of the zoo then is to maintain a back-up population in case a species becomes extinct in the wild,' Iona informed them. 'Unfortunately, though, there are still too many zoos around the world that treat their animals very badly.'

'The people who run those should be put behind bars and the animals set free,' said Aesha indignantly.

Joe shivered. The sun had gone in and he was beginning to feel cold. They packed up the picnic and continued their hike, circling back towards the jeep.

From one high point, they were able to look out across the sea, and it was then that Iona announced they would be spending the night in a log cabin on the shore. Joe was entranced at the prospect. *Wait till I tell my friends about this – this and the sniffer dogs*, thought Joe.

'We kept it as a surprise for you,' said Peter. 'Now you'll be able to say that you slept in the realm of the Amur tiger.'

'Won't it be freezing cold?' asked Aesha.

'Not if you keep the furnace stoked up,' said Iona. 'I'm going to drive back to the village with your mother to introduce her to our young vets, and we'll return in the morning. Tomorrow we'll check one or two of the camera traps, you'll stay here one more night, and then the next morning we'll return to the village to run through some of the films.'

'How do you decide where to put the cameras?' asked Aesha.

'From following their tracks we know the tigers' favoured routes,' said Iona. 'Like all cats, they mark their territory with their scent, usually on trees. We tie the cameras to trees that have been marked.'

'You mean trees that have wee on.' Joe giggled.

'Oh, Joe!' admonished Aesha. 'Trust you.'

'It's not wee, Joe,' Iona corrected him. 'It's a spray from their rear end or a rub from a facial scent gland.'

Joe pulled a face. Whatever it was, he didn't think it sounded very nice, but he still hoped that the cameras might show him a glimpse of a tiger.

Chapter 10

Joe was thrilled about staying in a log cabin on the beach.

'We'll be like Robinson Crusoe, won't we, Dad?' he said.

He was sure that this was where their holiday would turn into a real adventure, and had visions of fishing and collecting nuts and berries from the forest. He imagined a tumbledown shack and having to cook in front of it on an open fire.

The log cabin turned out to be simple but solidly built – and beautifully warm. A huge log-filled furnace provided heating and hot water. There was a very small kitchen with a wood-burning stove, a sitting area with several armchairs that had seen better days, and two bedrooms, one with bunk beds. Aesha groaned when she saw the bunk beds, complaining that she was far too old for that sort of thing. Joe quickly bagged the top one while she was still grumbling.

Peter decided it should be their job to keep the furnace stoked up and he would sort out the food. Joe chose to do the morning shift, since he liked to get up early, whereas his sister loathed leaving her bed.

'Just don't wake me up when you're clambering around at the crack of dawn,' she said, before agreeing to fetch the logs in the evening, though she argued that it shouldn't be a girl's job anyway.

'It'll be good for your fitness,' Peter said. 'And you can go for a swim beforehand if you like.'

Aesha groaned. 'You're so not funny, Dad.'

They all mucked in when they first arrived. Joe and his father fetched logs from a stack that had been neatly piled up by the side of the cabin, while Iona showed Aesha how to lay them in the furnace so that they caught fire quickly. Binti unloaded the provisions Iona had brought with her.

'I wish I was staying too,' Binti said. 'This looks really cosy.'

'Ah, the trials of being a highly sought-after wildlife vet,' sighed Peter dramatically. 'You miss out on so much.'

As soon as they were all set up, Binti and Iona departed for the park headquarters.

'And now the wicked father has been left to terrorise his poor children!' Peter adopted a witch's cackle.

'What are we supposed to do all evening?' Aesha pouted.

'You're going to sweep and clean and wash and cook and pander to your wicked father's every need. In between we'll eat a delicious meal and watch the sun go down.'

'It's nearly gone now, Dad,' said Joe, peering out through the window.

'We'd better go out and catch it quickly then,' said Peter. 'Wrap up warm.' He grabbed his coat and camera and headed for the door. Joe followed suit, with Aesha a little way behind.

The beach was made up of tiny pebbles. The sea was calm and reflected the red rays from the fading sun. All that could be heard were the gentle lapping of waves and a few strains of bird-song from the forest behind.

'Ah, peace!' Peter whispered, raising his camera to film the dusky sky and the reddening sea.

Joe faced in the opposite direction to take a shot of the moon hovering over the tops of the trees. As he lowered his camera, Aesha suddenly interrupted his thoughts.

'Shhh!' she said. 'Don't move. Look, Dad – over there!'

She was pointing towards a group of rocks a little distance away near the water's edge. A small fat animal with short legs and a round face was dipping its snout into a rock pool.

'What is it?' asked Joe. 'It looks like a sort of dog.'

Peter peered through the zoom lens of his camera. 'I know exactly what that is,' he said. 'It's a raccoon dog. Funny wee thing – it looks as if it's been put together out of the scraps left over from other creatures.'

'Is it dangerous?' asked Aesha.

'Only if you're a rodent or a fish,' her father replied. He took several photographs of the raccoon dog, before something frightened it and it scuttled away.

Joe was happy that they'd ended the day seeing an animal he hadn't even heard of before. It had been a great day, he decided, and Peter brought it to a close by dishing up a tasty dinner, which they ate by candlelight when the electricity cut out.

Chapter 11

'Dad! Come quickly, Dad!' Joe rushed back into the cabin. 'Come and look!'

It was early the next morning. Joe had gone to fetch logs for the furnace, which was burning low. It had snowed during the night and a light covering clung to the beach.

'What is it, Joe?' Peter appeared from his bedroom, yawning and shivering. 'Close that door – you're letting all the heat out.'

'Come and see,' Joe insisted.

'It had better be good,' Peter warned. 'I was having a wonderful dream about bumping into a bear and being invited back to his den for bangers and mash.'

'It is good. Hurry!'

As Peter put on his shoes, Aesha came out of the bedroom. She was bleary-eyed and decidedly grumpy.

'It's still dark,' she said. 'What's all the fuss about?'

'There's been a tiger!' said Joe. 'Come and look at the tracks.'

Peter followed him out of the cabin. A trail of prints ran from left to right, a sign that the animal that made them had stopped close to the cabin, perhaps to scratch itself, or to sit and rest. Peter bent down to study the prints, measuring one against the palm of his hand.

'Well!' he exclaimed. 'I'd say these were made by quite a large pussy cat.'

'Come inside and shut the door then!' cried Aesha. 'He might be waiting, ready to pounce!'

'Don't worry, my princess,' said Peter. 'The

prints go off into the distance. That tiger has gone somewhere else for breakfast.'

'I can't believe a tiger passed that close to us and we didn't see it,' said Joe. He was thrilled at his find, but cross that he hadn't been looking out of the window at the right time.

'We'll ask it to wear a bell around its neck next time, shall we?' joked his father.

'How can you stand there so calmly?' Aesha demanded.

'Don't worry – it's extremely rare for a tiger to attack a human,' said Peter. 'When it does happen, it's usually because the tiger has been provoked, or because injury or illness have affected its normal behaviour. I wouldn't have brought you here if I thought there was any danger.'

He ushered Joe back indoors and helped him to stoke the furnace, while Aesha went back to bed.

'Has that made your day?' he asked Joe.

Joe nodded. 'Mum and Iona will be amazed

when they find out. I hope the snow doesn't melt before they get here.'

'As soon as it's properly light, we'll take some photos as proof,' Peter promised. 'Something arty, I think. I shall do a series called "Tiger Dawn". If I'm lucky, the trees behind us will throw stripy shadows among the paw prints when the sun breaks through.'

'I'll call mine "Paw Prints in the Snow",' said Joe. 'And I'm going to stay up all night tonight in case the tiger comes back. This might be one of his favourite routes.'

Peter set to work making breakfast, a hearty affair of a sort of porridge followed by cold meats, boiled eggs, cheese and black bread. Tempted by the smells, Aesha reappeared, still grumpy from being woken too early and still anxious about their close encounter with a tiger.

'It's what we came here for, isn't it?' said Joe.

'I'm not fetching the logs tonight,' she stated firmly.

'You're scarier than the tiger.' Joe grinned at her, but she wasn't to be placated.

By the time Binti and Iona arrived in the middle of the morning, Joe and Peter had spent an hour or more wandering up and down the beach, following the trail of paw prints and taking photographs. Drawn by curiosity, Aesha had eventually joined them, though never straying too far from the cabin.

'You can even see where the claws are,' Joe said, delighted with his photographs.

Iona confirmed that the prints had been made by a male tiger and she was as excited as Joe at seeing them. 'If only he'd left some scat, we might have been able to identify him, but I suspect it was Misha. We've found evidence of him in this area before.'

Iona took a number of photographs herself and measured some of the paw prints, then announced that on the way back to Lazo Village they would drive to two of the camera traps to check they were functioning properly.

'More snow is forecast,' she explained, 'so I think it will be better for you to be in the village tonight rather than out here.'

Joe couldn't help but show his disappointment.

'I think we've been incredibly lucky so far,' Peter said, putting his arm around his shoulders. 'We've seen more than anyone could have expected.'

'I agree,' added Iona, 'and you never know what the camera traps might reveal.'

Chapter 12

They drove a long way that day, skirting the perimeter of part of the Lazovsky Nature Reserve and stopping occasionally for Iona to point out landmarks, or for Peter and Joe to take photographs. Joe was happy that they saw several deer and the tracks of a sable.

'A sable is like a pine marten,' Binti told him, 'or a large ferret.'

'There are lots in this part of the world,' said Iona. 'They used to be hunted in the wild for their fur, but now they're farmed for it instead.'

Aesha pulled a face. 'They shouldn't be farmed for their fur, either,' she objected. 'It's sick.'

'At least it protects the species that way,' said Iona. 'They might have died out otherwise.'

At last, they came to the first camera trap. Iona was pleased that it was still securely tied to a tree. She sniffed one of the trees close by, which made Joe giggle.

'Have a sniff if you want to know what tiger spray smells like.' She grinned at him.

'I can smell it from here,' said Aesha.

Joe bent down and inhaled. 'Pwah!' he cried. 'It stinks! Will there be photos of the tiger that did that?'

'Maybe,' said Iona. 'It all depends on which direction it passed by, although the ground around the camera tree looks quite disturbed. That means it may have stayed here for a while.'

'How does the camera work?' asked Aesha.

'It's got an infrared sensor which detects body heat close by and which activates it,' said Peter. He held his hand in front of the camera and it whirred into action.

'This one is quite old and only takes still

shots,' said Iona. 'Some of the newer ones take video footage.' She opened up the camera and replaced the film.

'Will we be able to watch you play it back?' Joe asked.

'We'll be doing that tomorrow, so if you've got nothing better to do . . .'

'Cool!' said Joe.

They piled back into the jeep and proceeded to the next trap, stopping on the way for a picnic lunch by a river. Once again, there were scent markings on trees surrounding the camera, but Iona discovered that it had been knocked and wasn't working properly. She took it down and checked it over.

'This happens sometimes,' she said. 'Animals can be quite aggressive with the strange boxes they find in their environment. We've got films where you can see a tiger butting the camera with its head or swiping it with its paw. I wonder how much we'll find has been shot on this film before the damage was done.'

It was already growing dark and the first snowflakes of the day were falling, so they returned to the jeep to begin the long drive back to the village.

'Tonight we'll eat in the café with some of the other workers, if that's all right with you,' Iona suggested. 'They'd love to meet two English children and have lots of questions to ask.'

Joe settled into his seat and watched the snowflakes dancing in the headlights. They were mesmerising, and as the evening closed in he found it difficult to stay awake. His mind played back the events of the day . . .

A trail of paw prints led him through a deep dark forest, where countless eyes followed his every move and where there was nowhere to hide. A tiger loomed in the distance, walking slowly, inexorably towards him, a gentle swagger disguising its fearsome power. Joe was terrified and bewitched at the same time. He wanted to flee, but he was rooted to the spot. And then the tiger strode straight through him as though he didn't exist.

Chapter 13

Joe really enjoyed the evening with the young vets and Nadia and the other fieldworkers. They wanted to know all about life in Britain; the weather, the food, football, school and, especially, the wildlife. They had heard that it rained all the time, that rich people lived in castles and that everybody kept cats and dogs. Joe and Aesha tried to put them right about a few things, but weren't convinced they always made themselves understood – much to everyone's amusement – even with Iona interpreting. Binti spoke about her local work in England as well as her international assignments, while Peter talked to them about some of the photographic projects he'd been involved in.

Joe was fascinated to hear more about the vets' work, and quickly realised that most of the time it involved sheer hard graft. It took hours of painstaking application and concentration to collect and analyse the data required to allow reasonable assumptions to be made both about the health of the tiger population and about the reserve as a whole.

'Once we've drawn conclusions from one set of results, we start the whole process again,' said Iona. 'Nothing stands still because the next set of data might produce different results. And all the time what we're looking for is evidence that tiger numbers and prey numbers are stable – if not growing.'

The young vets were impressed that, in the short time Joe and Aesha had been in Russia, they had already seen tiger tracks. It made Joe feel important, and he began to hope more and more that the film they had brought back from the camera trap would contain some good shots of tigers. He went to bed that night convinced that his tiger adventure had only just begun.

The following afternoon, when they headed into the viewing room, Joe just couldn't wait for the film to be downloaded.

'It's going to be so cool if there's a tiger on there,' he said to his mother, 'especially if there are cubs as well.'

Binti laughed. 'If there are, I think we'd better leave you out here as a lucky mascot!'

'What a good idea!' said Peter. 'No more smelly socks at home!'

The first two images came up on-screen. They were frustratingly blank. Iona explained that the camera was deliberately aimed at the mid-chest height of an average tiger, but could be triggered by the body heat of a smaller animal that wouldn't necessarily be within the camera's photographic range.

The next image was an indecipherable blur of dark brown.

'I think that might have been a wild boar in a hurry!' Iona chuckled.

Three more blank shots were followed by a very clear side view of another wild boar – or the same one on its way back, Iona suggested. Next came pristine images of the boar's snout, poised as though it were about to kiss the lens.

'Yuck!' said Aesha. 'It looks all wet and slobbery.'

'Don't be so rude about the poor thing,' Peter joshed.

'It looks healthy enough, doesn't it?' said Iona. 'And very interested to know if the camera is edible.'

There were a few more blank frames and then a roe deer was caught in a sequence of shots, seemingly posing at first, before nibbling at the leaves on a bush. Finally, a foot appeared at the top of one of the frames. It was black with very long claws.

'What's that?' squealed Joe excitedly.

'Wait and see,' said Iona.

The next two frames were completely black. The third was crossed by a black furry arm and a fourth revealed an ear. At last, a fifth frame showed the animal in its entirety as it dropped to the ground. It was an Asiatic black bear.

Joe couldn't believe his eyes. There were five more frames, all of them starring the bear, which was standing in the clearing in front of the camera, eating a nut from the tree.

'It's so cute!' said Joe.

'It looks like a right monkey to me,' said Peter.

'Funny, ha, ha, Dad,' said Aesha.

'They're not really very cute at all,' said Iona. 'There are quite a few bears in the reserve, and although they're herbivores, they can be pretty aggressive to humans. But they love acorns and they love climbing, so they climb up and try to grab them before they all fall to the ground and before other animals get to them.'

'The white stripe across its chest makes it look as if it's wearing a T-shirt.' Joe giggled.

'Or a bra,' said Aesha.

There was nothing else on the film, but seeing the bear made up for any disappointment Joe might have felt about the absence of a tiger.

Chapter 14

Joe and Aesha were left to their own devices the next day as Binti went to work with the vets and Peter decided to accompany her. Iona assured their parents that the village was perfectly safe for them to explore, and that the Museum of Nature was well worth a visit.

'We'll be back some time in the afternoon,' Binti said. 'Don't stray beyond the village, will you?'

'Don't fuss, Mum,' scoffed Aesha. 'We're used to looking after ourselves and I'm perfectly happy to chill for a day.'

Joe was keen to have a look at the exhibition of tiger paintings and the butterfly collection Iona had mentioned. He didn't want to go on his own, though. After some persuasion, Aesha agreed to accompany him, but as soon as they had seen all the exhibits she declared that she was tired and was going back to their room for a nap.

Joe decided it was a good opportunity to take some photographs since there would be nobody to hurry him on and he could spend time creating arty shots. *I'll surprise Dad with them*, he thought as he collected his camera and set off along the village streets.

Iona had told them that most of the villagers were farmers or hunters. Local children stared at him curiously or waved at him as he walked by, which made him feel very self-conscious, as though there were something different about the way he looked. He would have liked to take their photographs, but didn't dare in case he upset them. Instead, he took photographs of the park headquarters, the ferry, the old bus, the houses, the shops, the café and the museum.

As Joe was walking along one of the streets leading away from the village centre, he thought he saw a raccoon dog a little way ahead of him.

Wow! he said to himself. *Dad will definitely be impressed if I come back with a photo of a raccoon dog!*

He hurried after it. The animal began to run and Joe found it difficult to keep up on the slippery pavement. When he lost sight of it, he followed the tracks it had left in the snow. There were fewer and fewer houses now and the tracks were heading towards the forest.

That's so frustrating, Joe thought. *I was so close!*

He stopped and prepared to turn back.

It was probably only an ordinary dog anyway, he told himself.

Its legs had seemed a little too long for a raccoon dog, if he was honest. And snow was beginning to fall again, the sky thick and darkening.

Joe packed his camera into its case. At that very moment he heard an almost imperceptible, low growling noise coming from a dilapidated building set back from the road and apart from the nearest house.

Has the animal somehow found its way there? Joe wondered.

He decided to have one last attempt at photographing it.

If I were Dad, he said to himself, *I wouldn't let an opportunity like this go.*

He crept slowly over to the building, straining his ears for any noise that would give away the animal's position. The building looked unoccupied. With no further sounds to guide him, Joe approached the front, then stood and listened. There was silence apart from the rumble of a passing truck. He began to edge his way around to the back and was convinced he heard a slight scuffling. The ground to the rear sloped away quite steeply and Joe saw that there was a sort of basement to the building. Its entrance was marked by a crooked wooden door at the bottom of a steep flight of steps. Joe shivered in the gathering gloom, a wave of anxiety passing through him.

It's getting late. I really should return to the park headquarters.

He made up his mind to leave, but another, rather pathetic growl stopped him. It was coming from inside the basement, and whatever was making it seemed to be in trouble.

Joe went to the top of the steps, his heart beating fast. A small dog, even a raccoon dog, was nothing to be scared of, he reasoned. As the son of a vet, he would never be able to forgive himself for abandoning an injured animal. He would check that it was all right, then go home.

He put his foot on the first step, slipped on the ice and fell.

To his own ears, the scream Joe let out was loud enough to alert everyone in the village. He landed with a sickening thud in the courtyard in front of the basement door, his right leg twisted underneath him. He attempted to stand up, but couldn't. It was impossible – the pain was excruciating. As he tried to shift into a more comfortable position, it dawned on him that his leg might be broken.

Nobody knows where I am! The thought struck him like a hammer blow.

He called out for help, but his voice seemed thin and muffled by the falling snow. He pulled his coat tighter round him, glad that Binti had insisted they buy the thickest quilting on the market, whether or not Aesha complained about resembling a beluga whale in it.

Aesha will come and look for me, won't she? he thought. *She'll worry that I've been away for so long. Or is she fast asleep? Mum and Dad will finish work and be worried when they find I'm not back.*

Joe heard a growl, louder and more persistent than before. He hoped that whatever it was couldn't get out of the basement. He didn't want to be licked or slobbered over by a strange animal. And what if it bit him? What if the animal behind the door wasn't the small animal he had been following, but something bigger, perhaps one of the larger dogs he had seen wandering the village streets?

The pain became so intense that Joe started to feel light-headed. He knew he needed to stay awake, though, so he concentrated on calling out over and over again. He could hear cars passing once in a while, but no other sounds of human life.

He began to be scared that he might not be found for hours. What then? Even in his thick coat he would surely begin to suffer from the cold. He forced himself to think of everything they had done since they had been in Russia, every tiny detail, just to keep from falling asleep. He thought about the tiger tracks in the snow, the bear in the tree, the picnic by the waterfall, the day with the sniffer dogs and the way he had mistaken Artem Klopov for a smuggler. So much had happened in such a short space of time, and now his adventure had come to a disastrous end.

Chapter 15

Joe had no idea how long he lay there, the darkness closing in, the snow falling steadily. He was terrified that his tracks would be wiped out completely and that there would be no trace left of his last movements. He drifted in and out of consciousness, the pain eating away at his resolve to stay awake and the cold beginning to gnaw at both legs.

There had been no further sound from the animal in the basement. Joe wondered if it was still there, or whether it had managed to find a way out. When he heard a dog barking not too far away, he was convinced that the animal had made its escape from somewhere at the front of the building.

Joe thought about Foggy and wondered if he was still safely tucked up at Waggy Tails. He wanted to be with him now, lying alongside him, Foggy keeping him warm, licking his hand to keep him awake, protecting him from danger, barking frantically to alert his owners to their son's whereabouts.

The dog's barking grew louder and more insistent. It couldn't have been more than a few metres away. Joe was petrified. He curled into a ball and held his breath.

When the dog fell silent briefly, he heard the crunch of footsteps. *Footsteps!* A voice was issuing orders in Russian. Joe's heart beat faster. This might be his only chance of rescue.

'Help!' he cried as loudly as he could. 'HELP ME!'

The barking calmed down briefly, only to resume more loudly than ever. Joe wished it would stop so that whoever was with the dog would hear his cries.

'I'm here, behind the building,' he shouted. 'HELP ME!'

At last, he saw a beam of light moving around above him. Before he could call again, a large black dog hurtled down the steps, stopped briefly to sniff at him, then stood at the basement door, barking frantically and trying to find a way underneath it. The beam of light reached the top of the steps and fell on Joe.

'Help me, please,' he cried weakly. 'I think I've broken my leg.'

There was a gruff exclamation of surprise and someone came towards him.

'Joe?' asked a voice. 'Hurt?'

It was Artem Klopov. Joe had never been so relieved in all his life. He bit his lip hard, trying not to burst into tears, and nodded, pointing at his leg.

Artem bent down beside him. 'Look bad,' he said. 'Much pain?'

Joe nodded again. 'Were you looking for me?' he asked.

'I have my dinner and I take Boris for a walk,' Artem replied. 'Lucky I find you.'

Joe felt tearful again. 'Mum and Dad will be worried. They don't know where I am.'

'I think so,' said Artem. 'I tell them.'

Boris was still barking and scratching at the basement door. From inside came an aggressive roar, followed by a smaller growl of warning. Artem quickly stood up, listening.

'Tiger!' Artem said. 'You find tiger!'

'Tiger?' Joe couldn't believe what he was hearing.

'You find tiger. Boris find scent. Boris find you.'

'Tiger?' Joe said again. He still couldn't take it in.

'Good dog, Boris,' said Artem. 'He learn.'

'Do you mean there's a tiger behind that door?' Joe asked, incredulous.

Artem stood on tiptoe and shone his torch through the glass panel at the top of the door.

'Young male cub, I think,' he said. 'Not well.

91

I find help, for you, for him. I tell your mother and father so they not worry.'

Joe didn't want Artem to leave. He didn't want to be left on his own again, especially now he knew that the animal behind the door was a tiger. He had spent so many hours obsessed with the idea of seeing a wild tiger, but now that he was so close to one, he was scared it might get out, even if it was just a cub.

'I am quick,' Artem promised.

He clambered back up the steps, taking Boris with him.

Chapter 16

There's a tiger behind that door, Joe said to himself repeatedly. *I've been lying next to a tiger and I didn't even know.*

He knew he should have realised. There was the same acrid smell of spray that Iona had made him sniff in the reserve. He would have to sharpen up his act if he wanted to become a wildlife expert, or even a wildlife photographer. He shouldn't have missed such a big clue, broken leg or no broken leg.

To Joe's intense relief, Artem returned in no time with two men from the village, who brought with them blankets and a home-made stretcher. They gathered him up as gently as they could.

'Mother, Father, they come,' Artem assured him. 'You go hospital. Tiger too.'

Joe smiled weakly at the idea of the tiger going with him to hospital and lying in a bed alongside. Now that he was safe, he wanted to see the animal before they carried it away.

'Can I see him?' he asked. 'Can I see the tiger?'

Artem shook his head. 'Dangerous,' he said. 'Make him sleep first.'

The pain grew unbearable again, heightened by Joe's anxiety that the tiger might be taken away before he could even glimpse it. When his parents arrived at last, with Iona and a team of tiger experts, he couldn't help but sob at the feared loss of his last opportunity to see a tiger in the wild. He begged to be allowed to watch while the tiger was sedated before being moved from the basement.

Binti was distraught and wanted him to go straight to hospital.

'He's been lying here in the freezing cold for hours while we searched high and low. Who knows what might have happened if Artem hadn't found him when he did,' she said.

Peter, however, thought a few more minutes wouldn't do any harm. 'Ever since we arrived in Russia, our son's been obsessed with the idea of seeing a tiger. Let's not deprive him when he's so close to achieving his dream.'

'I suppose you're right,' Binti reluctantly agreed.

Joe could tell that she was shocked at what had happened to him and was blaming herself for not keeping a closer eye on him. 'I was following a raccoon dog,' he attempted to explain. 'I was about to turn back when I heard a noise coming from the basement ...'

From his stretcher, he looked on anxiously as one of the tiger experts placed a ladder against the door of the basement and climbed up it, carrying a gun.

'They're going to tranquillise him,' Peter told

him. 'Then your mother and the other vets will check him over before they take him away for treatment.'

Joe suddenly remembered his camera. 'Where's my camera, Dad?' he cried. 'Is my camera all right? I want to take a photo. Please let me take a photo.'

Artem handed Peter the camera case. 'Tough,' he said. 'Like Joe.'

'I hope so,' said Peter. He checked the camera over and passed it to Joe. 'I've got to hand it to you, Joe. I might have taken photos from some strange places, but this beats the lot!'

Joe smiled and felt a small glow of pride, then winced as the tranquilliser gun was fired.

Everyone waited quietly. After a few moments, when the all-clear was given, they opened the door and shone a light into the room. Joe raised his head and stared. There he was – the young Amur tiger he had unknowingly spent the last few hours with.

Joe was astonished at how big he was. When

Artem had told him it was a cub, he had imagined something the size of a terrier. This young tiger was more the size of an Old English sheepdog.

'He's so handsome!' Joe said. 'Look how big his paws are!'

He propped himself up against his father, raised his camera and pressed the button.

'Happy now?' Binti asked, stroking his hair.

Joe nodded and relaxed, keeping his eyes on the sleeping cub.

'He's about nine months old, I should say,' Iona told him. 'One month for every year of your life. He has an injured leg too. He must have become separated from his mother for some reason and strayed into the village, so he's had to fend for himself. He hasn't managed very well by the look of it.'

'Poor thing,' said Joe. 'What will happen to him now?'

'We'll take him to a rehabilitation centre, where he'll be given a thorough check-up.

Eventually, when he's fit and strong again, he'll be released back into the wild.'

'A little bit like you then, Joe,' joked his father.

'You know it was Boris who saved us, don't you?' Joe told Iona. 'He's not as slow on the uptake as you thought.'

Chapter 17

Joe's leg wasn't badly broken and he was allowed to leave hospital two days later. He was quite proud of the cast that stretched from his knee to his foot. Several of the hospital staff had written on it in Russian, wishing him a speedy recovery. The fieldworkers at the park headquarters wrote on it too, requesting that he visit them again in the future because he had brought them good luck. One of them even drew a tiger on it.

'We spend our lives tracking tigers and hoping for new ones to appear,' the fieldworker told him. 'You come here for a few days and – like magic – a cub we've never seen before arrives on our doorstep.'

Joe grinned. 'Perhaps it was because I wanted to see one so badly,' he said.

'And you think we don't!' the fieldworker replied.

The person Joe really wanted to sign his cast was Artem.

'So you've decided that walruses aren't so bad after all.' Peter grinned when Joe asked if he could meet up with him before they went back to England.

'He's cool,' said Joe.

He was delighted therefore when Iona called by later that day with Artem and Boris.

'Artem is a shy man and doesn't like a fuss,' said Iona, 'but he wants to say goodbye.'

Boris came bounding over to Joe, tail wagging furiously, but he sat obediently at a sharp word from his master.

'He's learning quickly,' remarked Joe.

'Leg come good?' Artem asked.

Joe nodded and thanked him. 'You saved my life,' he said.

Artem shrugged his shoulders. 'Not me,' he said. 'Boris.'

'The tiger is already making good progress,' Iona informed Joe. 'He was very thin and undernourished, but after a few good meals he'll be fine. Our main concern is that if his mother is no longer in the Lazovsky Nature Reserve, we may never know what happened to her.'

'So will the poor cub be all on his own when you release him?' Joe asked.

'Tigers are solitary animals once they're adults,' Iona replied. 'Unfortunately this cub is going to be on his own sooner than most, but we won't release him until he's ready. And we're very lucky to have your mother here for another three weeks, because she'll be helping the young vets to monitor his progress.'

Once again, Joe felt proud of his mother and the important work she did.

'When she leaves, please will you let us know how he gets on?' Joe begged.

'Of course,' Iona reassured him. 'And there's one more thing. The cub needs a name.'

Joe's heart skipped a beat. *Are they going to let me name him?*

'You tell him, Artem,' said Iona.

Joe held his breath and waited for Artem to speak.

'Tiger name – we call him … Joe,' Artem announced.

Joe couldn't believe his ears. Not only had he found a tiger in the wild, but the tiger had been named after him! He didn't think it was possible to feel happier and he would have jumped for joy if he could.

'Thank you!' he cried. 'Thank you, thank you, thank you!'

Just as Iona and Artem made to leave, Joe remembered why he had wanted to see Artem in the first place.

'Please will you sign my cast before you go?' he asked, holding out a pen.

A flicker of a smile lit up Artem's normally sombre face when he took the pen, before it disappeared again as he concentrated on the job in hand. While he was writing, Joe made a big fuss of Boris, and was reminded that Foggy would be waiting to greet them upon their return; Foggy, who had a nose for biscuits and not a lot else. Joe was looking forward to seeing him.

As soon as they had thanked Artem once more and said their goodbyes, Joe asked Iona what he had written.

'*Come back soon. Your friend, the Walrus!*' Iona read. 'I don't know what he means. Do you?'

Joe blushed bright red. 'It's a secret.'

Zoological Society of London

ZSL London Zoo is a very famous part of the
Zoological Society of London (ZSL).

For almost two hundred years, we have been working
tirelessly to provide hope and a home to thousands of
animals.

And it's not just the animals at ZSL's Zoos in
London and Whipsnade that we are caring for.
Our conservationists are working in more than
50 countries to help protect animals in the wild.

In Russia, Bangladesh and Indonesia we are fighting
to save the majestic and highly endangered tiger
through vital conservation projects.

But all of this wouldn't be possible without your help.
As a charity we rely entirely on the generosity of
our supporters to continue this vital work.

By buying this book, you have made an essential
contribution to help protect animals.
Thank you.

Find out more at **zsl.org/tigers**